For Charlotte, with my love

~ T C x

For my lovely friend Yvonne, and her mummy

~ A E

tiger tales

5 River Road, Suite 128, Wilton, CT 06897
Published in the United States 2013
Originally published in Great Britain 2013
by Little Tiger Press
Text copyright © 2013 Tracey Corderoy
Illustrations copyright © 2013 Alison Edgson
ISBN-13: 978-1-58925-130-4
ISBN-10: 1-58925-130-X
Printed in China
LTP/1800/0699/0413

3 5 7 9 10 8 6 4 2

For more insight and activities,
visit us at www.tigertalesbooks.com

I
Want
My
Mommy!

by Tracey Corderoy

Illustrated by Alison Edgson

tiger tales

Arthur was playing dragons when his mommy came in.

"Look, I'm flying!" Arthur giggled.

"Oh!" smiled Mommy. "What a busy little dragon! Are you ready to go to Grandma's house?"

"**Rargghh!**" roared Arthur grumpily.
"But I want to stay with YOU!"
He'd never been apart from Mommy
for the whole day before.

"You can show Grandma your dragon suit!" said Mommy. "You'll be *just* like her toy dragon, Huffity."

"Huffity!" Arthur cried. "I can play dragons with Huffity! Let's go!"

When they got to Grandma's house, Grandma gave Arthur a big hug.

"What a cute little dragon you are!" she said.

"Just like Huffity!" Arthur cried, and he ran inside to find him.

But soon it was time for
Mommy to go.
   Arthur held up his
little nose for a special
Mommy good-bye.
   "Rubby noseies,"
whispered Mommy.
   "Rubby noseies,"
sniffed Arthur.

Then he waved and
waved until Mommy
was gone.

"Would you like to paint
a picture?" Grandma asked, but
Arthur just wanted Mommy.
"**Rargghh!**" he grumped.
"Dragons don't paint!"

"Or we could make dragon music?" smiled Grandma, banging on a drum.

"OK!" said Arthur. Dragons *did* like drums.

But then . . .

ding - dong!

went the doorbell.

"**Mommy's back!**" Arthur cried.

But it *wasn't* his mommy.

"**Rargghh!**" grumped Arthur.

"Dragons don't want LETTERS!"

"It's all right," said Grandma softly. "Mommy will be back later."

Arthur gave a little dragon sniff.

"Look, Arthur!" said Grandma. "I've got some treasure. But I need a brave dragon to protect it."

"Me!" cried Arthur. "I'm brave!" He would hide it in a cave.

He ran into the backyard to find one.

When Arthur had found the perfect dragon cave, he sat in it with the treasure.

"Hee hee!" he giggled. No one would find it here!

Then suddenly, he heard another . . .

ding-dong!

"**Mommy!**" cried Arthur,
running inside.

But it was just Grandma's friend, returning an umbrella. "**Rargghh!**" grumped Arthur. "Dragons don't want UMBRELLAS!"

"I think it's lunchtime," Grandma said.
They sat together at the table.

"Mommy will be back very soon,"
smiled Grandma. "But until she gets here,
I know a game we can play!"

Grandma put a towel around her shoulders.
"Look, I'm a knight!" she cried.
"This is my cape!"
"And this is my sword!"
"Wow!" Arthur gasped.
"Hey, I want to find some
treasure!" Grandma-Knight
smiled.

"**Rargghh!**" giggled
Arthur-Dragon. "You
won't get mine!"

He raced to his cave to protect
his shiny treasure.
   "Grandma-Knight's coming to
catch you!" Grandma chuckled.

"Hee heeeeee!" squealed
Arthur, as she tickled his tummy.
Then they played knights and
dragons all afternoon, until . . .

ding-dong!

"I hope they're not looking for treasure!" laughed Arthur and Grandma, running to the door.

"**Rargghh!** I'm a brave dragon and you can't come in!" giggled Arthur.

But, when the door opened . . .

"**Mommy!**"
cried Arthur.
And Mommy gave
Arthur a great big hug!

"Did you have fun?" she asked him.
"Lots and lots!" said Arthur.
"Dragons love playing with their grandmas so much. But *no one* gives hugs like Mommy!"